CREDO

Communion Service in E

4

Son of God._____

Son_____ of God. Be-got-ten of his___ Fa - ther_____ be-fore

all worlds, God of God,_____ Light of__ Light, Ve - ry God of

ve - ry God, Be - got-ten, not_____ made, Be-ing of one sub-stance with the

Man.

Oxford Church Services

General Editor David Willcocks

OXFORD UNIVERSITY PRESS · MUSIC DEPARTMENT · 44 CONDUIT STREET · LONDON, WIR ODE

S550
S.A.T.B.

25p

For King's College, Cambridge

COMMUNION SERVICE IN E
(Collegium Regale)

HAROLD DARKE

KYRIE

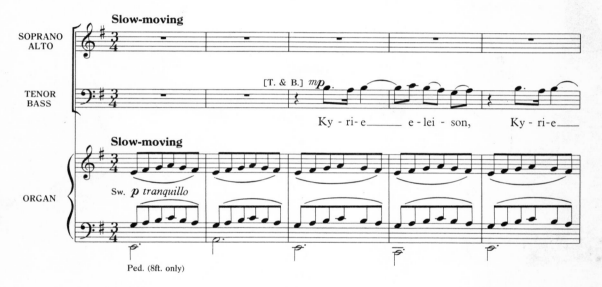

Printed in Great Britain

2

6

And was made_____ man, And was cru-ci-fied al-so for us_____ un-der

Pon - tius Pi - late. He suf-fered_____ and was bur-ied,_____

Allegro

And the third day he_____ rose a-gain_____ ac-cord-ing to the

And the third day he_____ rose a-gain_____

Communion Service in E

Communion Service in E

SANCTUS

BENEDICTUS

-san - na in the high - est. Ho- san - na in the high - - - est. A - - - - men.

AGNUS DEI

O Lamb of God, that ta - kest a - way the sins of the world, have

Communion Service in E

14

mer - cy up - on us. O Lamb of God, that ta - kest a - way the

sins___ of the world, have mer - cy up - on us.

O Lamb of God, that ta - kest a - way___ the sins,___ the

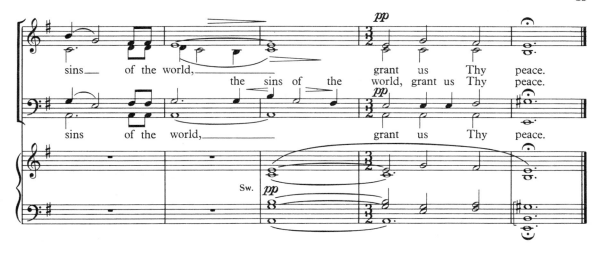

GLORIA

Communion Service in E

16

praise thee, we bless thee, we wor - - - - - ship thee, we glo - ri - fy

thee. We give thanks to thee for thy great glo - - - - -

- - ry, O Lord God,___ Heav'n - ly King,_____

God the Fa-ther Al-migh-ty.   O

Lord, the on-ly be-got-ten Son,   Je-su Christ; O Lord   God,

Lamb of God,   Son of the Fa-ther, that ta-kest a-way— the sins

Communion Service in E

SOPRANOS

of the world, have mer - cy up - on us. Thou that

Man.

ta - kest a - way the sins of the world, have

Ped.

SOPRANOS
p espress.

mer - cy up - on us. Thou that ta - kest a - way the

p

Man.

Communion Service in E

20

in the glo-ry of God the Fa - - ther.

[S. & A.]
A - men. A - men. A - - men.

[T. & B.]

allargando

After the blessing.
Slow
A - - - - - - - men.

A - - - - - - men.

VOICES and ORGAN

A - - - men.

A - - - men. A - - - men.

Processed and printed by
Halstan & Co. Ltd., Amersham, Bucks., England

OXFORD UNIVERSITY PRESS

Oxford University Press

publications for the church musician

Choirs have for many years used the famous *Oxford Anthems* and *Oxford Easy Anthems*. These two series, which are now edited by David Willcocks, provide a wide range of anthems, the majority of which are by contemporary composers.

The *Oxford Church Services* series, also edited by David Willcocks, contains many interesting new settings of the Canticles and of the Communion Service.

The separate issues of *Tudor Church Music* include many of the greatest works of the period. Revised editions, which take account of the latest advances in scholarship, are published at regular intervals.

Oxford University Press acts as publisher to the *Church Music Society*. The selected works published by the Society are of the greatest interest and value.

As well as vocal music, the Oxford University Press publishes much *Music for Organ*, with and without pedals. The albums of collected pieces—some for special occasions, others for general use—are worthy of particular note, many containing fine examples of both early English and modern music.

Details of all works for choirs, including a number of cantatas and other works not in any of the series listed above, are given in the catalogues 'Oxford Church Music' and 'Oxford Music for Christmas'. Details of all publications for organ are given in the catalogue 'Oxford Organ Music'. Copies of these catalogues will be sent without charge on request.

London   New York   Toronto

27.12.68

ISBN 0 19 351576 8